This book belongs to

First published by Red Panda, an imprint of Westland Publications Private Limited, in 2021

Published by Red Panda, an imprint of Westland Books, a division of Nasadiya Technologies Private Limited, in 2025

No. 269/2B, First Floor, 'Irai Arul', Vimalraj Street, Nethaji Nagar, Alapakkam Main Road, Maduravoyal, Chennai 600095

ISBN: 9789360451332

10 9 8 7 6 5 4 3 2 1

Printed at Thomson Press (India) Ltd

Mermaids in the Moonlight

These stories from the waters of the world are offered with respect and honour for the peoples, cultures, languages and places that they originate from.

SHARANYA MANIVANNAN

My name is Nilavoli.

My amma named me for the moon and its light.

Amma promised to take me to the Mattakalappu lagoon as soon as I was old enough to always remember it. She told me how, on full moon nights, if you dipped an oar or a paddle into the lagoon and held its other side to your ear, you could hear mysterious sounds coming from deep underwater. She would say it was a mermaid, singing.

We flew to the island and then drove for a very long time, until we finally arrived at the mermaid arch at the entrance of Mattakalappu.

On the next night, as the full moon rose above us, we went to the Kallady lagoon.

Our guide, Raju uncle, helped us onto the motorboat. We didn't need oars, except to listen to the underwater sounds. He gave us bright-orange life vests to wear, but I didn't want to, until he said, 'Thangachi, this is for your safety. The sea is full of mysteries. Years ago, I saw a tsunami rise over those coconut trees on the horizon, and smash into us. It shattered so many of our lives.'

'There's a lot of sorrow in this place,' Amma whispered to me. 'Sometimes you just have to pause and feel it.'

Amma was already a grown-up when she first came to the lagoon. Her family had left the country when she was a small girl because there had been a war. She had also heard about the singing mermaid for a long time before she actually ...

... heard her!

Raju uncle stopped the motor. Amma held me as I dipped my oar into the water and listened to the melodious sound of ...

... frogs?

Amma laughed. 'Don't be disappointed—it's not a woman's voice you'll hear. No one knows for sure who or what makes this music, but Mattakalappu might be the only place in the world where you can hear it. Scientists say that the sounds come from a type of shell, from the way the underwater currents touch them, or from creatures that live inside them. Some also say there are types of **"singing fish"**.

'Then there are dreamers like you and me who want to believe there can be mermaids in the lagoon. Fish-tailed, with a human heart.'

Raju uncle took us to another spot on the water. Here, I could hear a humming sound ...

Amma said, 'Doesn't this remind you of when we listened to the recordings of imploding pulsar stars in deep space?'

'I wonder how many mermaids there must be, to make all these different noises in the lagoon. They say that over a hundred years ago, the sounds used to be so loud that you needn't even enter the lagoon or dip your oar in the water! You could hear them as you walked along the banks or on a bridge. Some even say the sound was like a rudra veena, a stringed musical instrument. Or maybe it was like a yazh, an ancient Tamil harp?'

I began to feel better. I understood that there were so many ways to listen to these sounds.

'Maybe it's the mermaid's tummy rumbling,' I giggled. 'She must be hungry!'

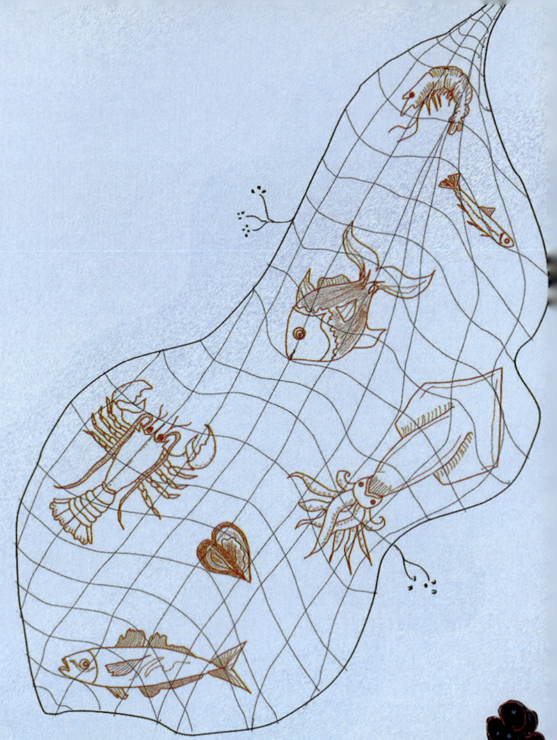

'I wonder if our mermaid is singing all the time,' said Amma. 'Maybe she sings softly at other times, but when the moon is full, she calls out to us.'

'Does she have a name, Amma?' I asked.

Amma smiled, looking into the distance. The wind played with her hair. 'The water and the moon have an old, old love for each other,' she said. 'Why don't we call her "Ila"? Because it's inside "Nila", or "moon", which is inside "Nilavoli", your name. And it's also half of "Ilankai", the Tamil name for this island ...'

The waves lapped at the side of the boat. 'Tell me her story, Amma.'

A cloud moved over the moon. It was too dark to see if Amma was still smiling, but I could hear her smile in her voice and feel it in the way she squeezed my hand. 'I don't know if Ila has her own story, kunju,' she said. 'Maybe she once did. There are so many stories that disappear, like tears underwater ...

'But our planet is made mostly of oceans and rivers. And there have been so many mermaids across the world's waters.

'The sea has its own music. Sound moves differently underwater. Did you know, humpback whales also have songs? They learn new ones as they travel around the world.'

'Imagine all the stories they would know!' I said.

'Yes!' Amma laughed. 'I can tell you a few that I know ...'

'Far, far away, in a land without a sea, a royal mermaid, Mélusine of Luxembourg, liked to be a human most of the time. When she married a nobleman, she kept her true self a secret. But she made a rule that every Saturday, she would spend time alone, doing whatever she wanted.

'One Saturday, her husband spied on her.

'He was shocked to find her splashing happily in a bathtub, with two tails!'

'In Brazil, Saturday is the special day of the goddess Yemanjá. She swam across the Atlantic Ocean centuries ago, comforting the people of West Africa who were enslaved and taken from their homelands on ships. Her first home is the Ogun river, but she rises wherever there are cowrie shells and white roses, and someone who longs for her.

'She lets our pain dissolve into saltwater, in the sea and in our tears.'

'Sedna of the Arctic Circle married a sea-bird, disguised as a man. He promised to be good to her but he wasn't. One day, her father visited them. She begged him to help her escape. He did, but still angry with her for leaving him, he threw her over the boat when the ferocious sea-bird chased them! She clung to the boat desperately, but he chopped off her hands, which turned into sea creatures. Sedna drifted to the bottom of the ocean and became its great goddess. Because she has no hands, she cannot comb or braid her hair. Sometimes she becomes lonely or upset, and then the water-hunters have empty nets. This is when wise shamans travel to her and stay beside her, untangling the knots in her long, seaweed-like hair. They show her how cherished she is.'

'Ancient fish-tailed deities like Atargatis and Oannes were once worshipped in West Asia. There were many stories there about sea monsters and aquatic creatures. Some underwater beings, like Julnar the sea-born, even had legs and could choose to live on land—as long as they took a swim now and then! Julnar married a king on land. When she had a baby, Badr Basim, she took the newborn deep into the sea, so that he would always feel at home in both worlds. His name means "smile of the full moon"!'

'Speaking of moons again ...

... Dogon people in Mali understood complex astronomy centuries ago. They say it's because Nommo, mermaid-like beings, came from outer space and taught them.

'In another part of the same continent, in the dry, almost desert-like Klein Karoo region of South Africa, there are ancient rock paintings of mermaids.'

'Menana, a girl from the Ottawa Nation, loved to look up at the night sky. She wanted to shine like the stars. Her wish was granted. She shimmered in the sky for a long time.

'But she grew bored and longed to be a girl again. This was not possible immediately. First, she would have to be a flood-spirit. So, for some time she was **half-girl** and **half-fish**, splashing in waterfalls and pools with joy.

'One day, she became fully human-bodied, but the time she had spent with the constellations and the water-beings meant that she could always know and see many worlds at once.'

As Amma spoke, it felt like even the moon was leaning in to listen sometimes ...

'I love stories in which mermaids get their heart's desire! In Cornwall, they are called "môr-forwyn" and the coasts are full of their lore. People still see them sitting on rocks, untangling their hair with shell combs and gazing into mirrors that catch the sunlight. There was one named Morveren who loved to listen to a man's beautiful singing in the ancient church of St Senara (some say St Senara was a môr-forwyn too!). Each time she heard his voice rising in the wind, she would come closer and closer to the land, until one day she came right up to the church.

'When the singing man saw her, he knew he wanted to belong to her always. Together, they entered the waters—and yes, lived happily ever after ...'

'Sailors who saw mermaids through telescopes sometimes got closer and saw they were dugongs or manatees instead. But what if they were both mermaids and mer-creatures? The singing whales might tell tales—or should that be tails?—about selkies who rise out of the European seas as seals, uncloak their skins, and walk around as human women. Selkies move between two worlds, using their fins or feet.

'They love this freedom to be themselves in different ways. But sometimes, men who want to keep them bound in one place steal their skins and hide them. In these stories, the selkie always has a secret wish deep in her heart, no matter how long she lives on land. And as soon as she finds her stolen skin, she slips into it, dives into the nearest body of water and returns home.'

'The Hawai'ian goddess Moana-Nui-Ka-Lehua lived as a shark sometimes. In those islands are many kinds of beings known as mo'o. The word "mo'o" means "lizard", because of the way they can shed their tails.

'This reminds me of another kind of mermaid, the karukayn, from Gurindji country. She can remove her tail whenever she wishes to and use her legs, which are inside it!'

'Let me also tell you about some humans who live in water ...
The Bajau Laut people of South East Asia have lived in the sea and on houseboats for so many generations that their bodies have evolved. Their spleens, which help release oxygen into the blood, are much larger than ours (sea mammals also have larger spleens). Their vision is sharper. They can dive **deeper**, and stay in the depths longer than most humans.

'Long ago, men would descend into the Gulf of Mannar, between Ilankai and India, to find **pearls** and **conches**. The waters were dangerous, so shark-charmers who could predict the movements of sharks through prayer were important people.

'In Japan, women who are called "ama" dive for pearls. They wear white and sacred symbols to protect them underwater.

'Women on Jeju Island dive to collect **sea-harvest** of all kinds. Known as "jamnyeo", they are strong, older women who are the heads of their households. They make high whistling sounds underwater through a breathing technique known as "**sumbisori**", that they learned from observing whales and seals. Or maybe, long ago, the mer-creatures told them their secrets ...

'Women also dive for seaweed in Rameshwaram in India, which is the land point closest to Ilankai. Over the years, so many people tried to make the crossing on tiny boats, to escape the war and the pain here ...'

'Remember the tsunami? It happened because of an undersea earthquake in the Indian Ocean. The goddess Nyai Ratu Blorong controls the waves of the waters of the Nusantara region, where the calamity began.

'She loves shadow puppetry, mirrors, batik fabrics and the edible nests of salanganen birds, gathered from dangerous cliffs by the Java Sea. She also loves the colour aquamarine green so much that it makes her angry if anyone else wears it! She's connected to the moon, too. When it's full, she looks young, and when it isn't, she appears to be a wise and old woman. She is both caring and ferocious, just as oceans are.

'Mermaids are often like this—full of power that can be kind or that can hurt. They can be moody, just like the sea. In the Chiloé islands, when La Pincoya dances watching the sea, small creatures will gather together and be easy to catch. If she looks at the mountain instead, they will scatter, and the sea-harvest will be poor. Along with her sister, La Sirena Chilota, and her brother, Pincoy, she guides the spirits of drowned sailors ...

'In Eastern Europe, you must be careful if you ever meet a rusalka, a mer-spirit who haunts lakes and swamps restlessly. They say that every rusalka is a sad soul who wants to spread her sorrow. There is a story about an engkantada, in the Philippines, who destroyed an entire village after the eggs she had laid were stolen. (Yes, I suppose some mermaids do lay eggs, like fish!) In the Jaintia Hills is a water deity so powerful that some say it is forbidden to speak her name.

'There are stories about fair punishments, too. The ningyo of Japan have a curse of immortality in their flesh, and those who eat them find out how difficult it is to live forever. In the pools of Perranzabuloe is a mermaid who seeks justice for women and girls who have suffered, by dragging evildoers into the deep swirling waters ...'

'What do they look like? The people who have seen them, or felt the tide that rises when the mermaids summon it, say different things. It doesn't matter; what we know is that they are somehow magical ...'

Amma was thoughtful suddenly. 'I am not sure, you know, what our Ila may be like. This place has seen so much ...'

We were quiet for a moment.

Crick crick croo ...

Under the water, the music continued.

'Remember the yazh, the ancient musical instrument? Vipulananda Adigal, a famous teacher from here in Mattakalappu, wrote a book about it. He also wrote songs about the meen magal, a Tamil word for mermaid.

'There were other Tamil writers who wrote about a continent called Kumari Kandam which sank beneath the sea. Some say it was ruled by women. Can you imagine if they evolved fins and gills and tails as their world became submerged?

'There's definitely a deep connection between mermaids and music. In Peru and Bolivia, guitar-like instruments known as charangos are made in a mermaid shape and left in places where the la sirenita can bless them, so the ones who play them can make their listeners fall in love!'

'A part of Ilankai is named Yazhpanam, after the yazh! That brings me to a beautiful story about a mermaid in those northwestern waters. Suvarnamaccha, whose name means "golden fish", was a daughter of Ravana, the king of Lanka. She was the leader of an army of mermaids.

'This story is actually from Thailand! Isn't it amazing how a story can travel, just like a coconut that can float its way from shore to shore?'

'Hanuman and his army of monkey-men were trying to build a bridge to Ilankai from India, to rescue Sita, who was being held captive. Every night, he noticed that the rocks that formed the bridge were gone. One night, he hid and waited, and met Suvarnamaccha. They fell in love, and she agreed to help him.'

(I imagined what her golden scales would be like, shimmering in the light of the sun and the moon whenever she surfaced to meet him.)

As we sat there in the boat, Amma told me tale after tale about mermaids, mer-creatures and marine spirits.

They swam everywhere in the world—

in still lakes and rushing waterfalls,

cosy bathtubs and immense oceans,

in underground caverns, oases, cenotes

... and more

—anywhere with a little room to splash around!

'For centuries, fishing was a very important trade for the people of Mattakalappu. Women led many families. The lands and houses belonged to mothers and were passed on to daughters. If they married, the men would move into the women's homes.

'So what I think is that the mermaid—half-fish and half-woman—contains both the symbols that were most important to the people of this place, which is half-land and half-lagoon.'

Like this, we drifted on the lagoon, with the dark openness of the sea on one side, and the city lights and two bridges on another.

And every now and then, we would stop and dip our oars into the lagoon ...

and listen …

This time, I could see Amma's soft eyes glinting in the night just like the reflection of electrical lights on the lagoon's waves. I was a baby when Amma became mine, when the adoption centre sent us to each other.

'No matter where you are in the world, and no matter how old you are ...' she began, '... on full moon nights, remember to look up at the sky.

'The moon's face will remind you of these mermaids, this lagoon, this island—and of me. These are all your own true stories.'

We dipped our oars back into the water one last time. I closed my eyes and tried to memorise the music of this night. And then Raju uncle switched the boat's motor on again, and it was time to return to land.

Amma told me once that there is another way to say my name, and that means 'moon's sound'. Now that I have listened to Ila and the other mermaids of the Mattakalappu lagoon, how they called to me in silences and scratchy noises like star-songs, it makes me wonder what the moon's song may be ...

A NOTE

Ilankai and Mattakalappu are the Tamil names of places you may know as Sri Lanka and Batticaloa. The mysterious sounds that rise in the lagoon during full moon nights are real.

As for Ila, the mermaid of Mattakalappu, she is imagined by Nilavoli and Amma, and they hope you will imagine her with them too!

Amma tells Nilavoli some mermaid stories that she has read or heard. We must always remember that there are stories underneath stories, and some that we will never know. Stories may belong to the world, but when they travel, they sometimes change. Nilavoli, Amma and Ila hope this book inspires you to learn more about different versions of stories, and the peoples and cultures that they originally came from.

About the Author and Illustrator

Sharanya Manivannan is the author of the beloved picture book *The Ammuchi Puchi* (illustrated by Nerina Canzi). She also writes fiction and poetry for adults, including *The Queen of Jasmine Country* and *The High Priestess Never Marries.*

Mermaids In The Moonlight is her debut as an illustrator, and is followed by a graphic novel for adults, Incantations Over Water.